I FEEL YOU

Written By: Kinyel Friday
Illustrated By: Robert Roberson, Jr.

RATTLED

TIRED

OVERWHELMED

STRESSED

Jasmine wakes up to the sun shining in her face, but then discovers that her alarm clock is flashing angry red numbers at her. OH NO! She knows what that means. The power went out during the night! AND she's going to be late for school if she doesn't hurry!

CONFIDENT
VICTORIOUS
PROUD
overjoyed

There are four seconds left in the game. Brandon steals the ball, dribbles down the court, and scores for the win! His team now gets to play in the championship game next week. The crowd goes crazy!

ECSTATIC
blissful
Marvelous
playful

Monica puts on her new birthday dress and twirls around. She feels like a princess. All she needs is a unicorn to take her on a ride!

HOPEFUL
DEFEATED
uncertain Calm

Xavier gets his test back and there's a big B+ on the front. It is far from failing, but he knows he studied hard for that test and thought he would earn an A. He talks to his teacher to find out what he did wrong.

ANXIOUS GUARDED

Vanessa picked a movie for family movie night but had no idea how scary it would be! She has her parents check for monsters under her bed and in her closets.

FRIGHTENED CAREFUL

GLOOMY
ENVIOUS
UPTIGHT *jealous*

During recess, Wesley can't help but to stare at his best friend's shoes. He wishes he had new shoes too; he can't remember the last time he had a new pair.

KiND

valued

zealous

needed

Kiana and her mom volunteer at their church on the weekends. They love to give back to their community by helping other people.

SPREAD A LIL' KINDNESS

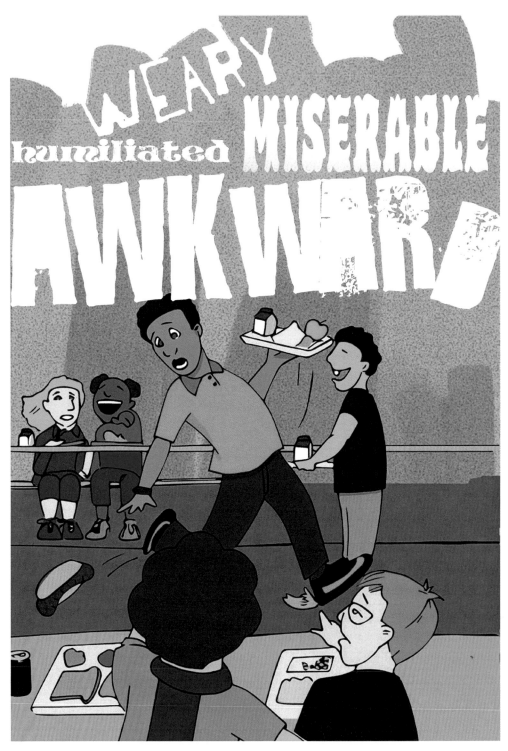

Chris slips and his hot dog falls on the floor before he reaches the lunch table. Everyone turns around and laughs. How embarrassing!

betrayed
IRRITABLE BOTHERED
HORRIFIED

Talaya is accused of stealing her friend's charm bracelet. Her friend's mother calls to ask for it back. Her friend, Olivia, broke the bracelet and was too afraid to tell her mother.

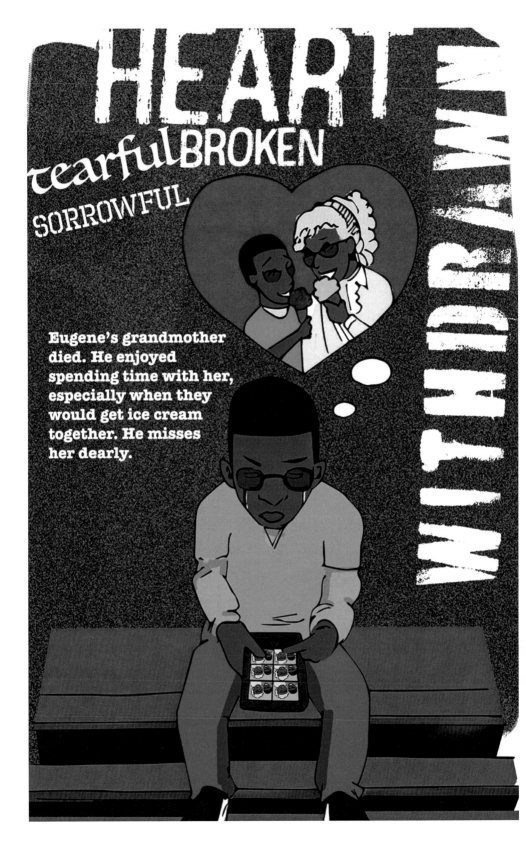

HEART

tearful BROKEN

SORROWFUL

WITHDRAWN

Eugene's grandmother died. He enjoyed spending time with her, especially when they would get ice cream together. He misses her dearly.

JOYFUL
EAGER
Delighted
impatient

Raquel can't wait to go on her school trip to the zoo.
Her favorite animal is the cheetah, and she also loves
visiting the aquarium.

Quinton volunteers to present his poem at his school's honor roll assembly. He loves to write in class and wants to be a teacher when he grows up.

Pam lost her book at the airport. The next day, the book is on her bed. Pam thinks her mom bought her a brand new one.

Bashful
DISAPPOINTED

INSECURE   *lonely*

Nikki's first day of school is not what she expected. All of her friends are in other classes, and she doesn't know anyone in her class.

FaIR

sociable
thoughtful
WARM

Dion likes to share his toys with his friends when they come over. If they are still there at dinnertime, his friends eat with Dion's family.

Sometimes it's hard to figure out how we truly feel. We all have different feelings, and it is healthy to use our words to express them. But if we hold our feelings in or act out instead of using our words, that's when our behavior becomes inappropriate — not the feeling itself. So, remember to use your words.

There are plenty of them!

DICTIONARY

All feeling words from the story are used as adjectives.

Amused:
Feeling pleasantly entertained.

Anxious:
Feeling extreme uneasiness or fear.

Awkward:
Feeling lack of ease or grace.

Bashful:
Feeling socially shy.

Betrayed:
Feeling mistreated.

Blissful:
Feeling full of happiness.

Bothered:
Feeling worried or annoyed.

Brave:
Feeling the strength to face fear or danger.

Calm:
Feeling free from excitement.

Careful:
Feeling cautious.

Confident:
Feeling certain or sure of yourself.

Defeated:
Feeling frustrated or a loss.

Delighted:
Feeling highly pleased.

Determined:
Feeling set with a decision.

Disappointed:
Feeling let down or having your hopes dashed.

Eager:
Feeling an impatient desire or interest.

Ecstatic:
Feeling an overwhelming happiness.

Envious:
Feeling jealous.

Fair:
Feeling you have acted in an honest way.

Frightened:
Feeling fearful.

Fulfilled:
Feeling happiness.

Giddy:
Feeling lighthearted and silly.

Gloomy:
Feeling sad.

Grateful:
Feeling thankful.

Guarded:
Feeling a need to be careful.

Guilty:
Feeling bad for doing something wrong.

Heartbroken:
Feeling extremely sad.

Hopeful:
Feeling full of hope.

Horrified:
Feeling shocked.

Humiliated:
Feeling embarrassed.

Impatient:
Feeling restless.

Insecure:
Feeling unsure.

Irritable:
Feeling easily angered.

Jealous:
Feeling envious or suspicious.

Joyful:
Feeling happy.

Kind:
Feeling helpful.

Lonely:
Feeling alone.

Loved:
Feeling really liked.

Marvelous:
Feeling wonderful.

Miserable:
Feeling extremely unhappy.

Needed:
Feeling necessary or wanted.

Nervous:
Feeling uneasy.

Overjoyed:
Feeling extremely happy.

Overwhelmed:
Feeling overcome.

Playful:
Feeling full of fun.

Proud:
Feeling pleased with yourself.

Rattled:
Feeling upset.

Relieved:
Feeling relief.

Safe:
Feeling secure or unhurt.

Shy:
Feeling easily scared.

Sociable:
Feeling friendly with others.

Sorrowful:
Feeling grief or sadness.

Stressed:
Feeling overwhelmed.

Tearful:
Feeling like crying.

Thoughtful:
Feeling considerate of others.

Tired:
Feeling drained or without
energy.

Uncertain:
Feeling unsure.

Uptight:
Feeling nervous or angry.

Valued:
Feeling important.

Victorious:
Feeling fulfilled or like you won.

Warm:
Feeling friendly and affectionate.

Weary:
Feeling tired or worried.

Withdrawn:
Feeling removed or shy.

Zealous:
Feeling excited or energetic.

Children's Books by Kinyel Friday

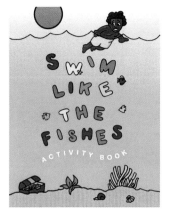 

Other Books by Kinyel Friday
Troubled Minds (short story)

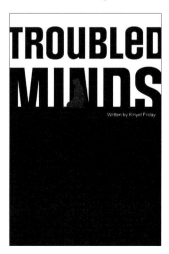

I FEEL YOU

Published by
KinYori Books, LLC
46036 Michigan Avenue, #283
Canton, MI 48188

KinYori
BOOKS

Made in United States
North Haven, CT
17 September 2022

24249267R00015